George Melville Baker

Above the Clouds

George Melville Baker

Above the Clouds

ISBN/EAN: 9783337341862

Printed in Europe, USA, Canada, Australia, Japan

Cover: Foto ©Andreas Hilbeck / pixelio.de

More available books at **www.hansebooks.com**

Plays for Amai

BY GEORG‘ ?

Author of "Amateur Dramas," " The Mimic St.
Stage," " Handy Dramas," " The Exhu...

Titles in this Type are Ne.

Titles in this Type are Tempera..

GEO. M. BAKER & CO., 41-45 Franklin St., Boston.

Just Published. The "Popular Edition" of Baker's Reading Club and Handy Speaker. Nos. 1, 2, 3, and 4, 50 selections in each. Price 15 cents each.

ALL THE WORLD'S A STAGE.

THE AMATEUR DRAMA.

ABOVE THE CLOUDS.

BOSTON:
GEO. M. BAKER & CO.,
Nos. 41-45 Franklin Street.

SPENCER'S UNIVERSAL STAGE.

A Collection of COMEDIES, DRAMAS, and FARCES, adapted to either Public or Private Performance. Containing a full description of all the necessary Stage Business.

PRICE, 15 CENTS EACH. ☞ No Plays exchanged.

1. **Lost in London.** A Drama in Three Acts. 6 Male, 4 Female characters.

2. **Nicholas Flam.** A Comedy in Two Acts. By J. B. Buckstone. 5 Male, 3 Female characters.

3. **The Welsh Girl.** A Comedy in One Act. By Mrs. Planche. 3 Male, 2 Female characters.

4. **John Wopps.** A Farce in One Act. By W. E. Suter. 4 Male, 2 Female characters.

5. **The Turkish Bath.** A Farce in One Act. By Montague Williams and F. C. Burnand. 6 Male, 1 Female character.

6. **The Two Puddifoots.** A Farce in One Act. By J. M. Morton. 3 Male, 3 Female characters.

7. **Old Honesty.** A Comic Drama in Two Acts. By J. M. Morton. 5 Male, 2 Female characters.

8. **Two Gentlemen in a Fix.** A Farce in One Act. By W. E. Suter. 2 Male characters.

9. **Smashington Goit.** A Farce in One Act. By T. J. Williams. 5 Male, 3 Female characters.

10. **Two Heads Better than One.** A Farce in One Act. By Lenox Horne. 4 Male, 1 Female character.

11. **John Dobbs.** A Farce in One Act. By J. M. Morton. 5 Male, 2 Female characters.

12. **The Daughter of the Regiment.** A Drama in Two Acts. By Edward Fitzball. 6 Male, 2 Female characters.

13. **Aunt Charlotte's Maid.** A Farce in One Act. By J. M. Morton. 3 Male, 3 Female characters.

14. **Brother Bill and Me.** A Farce in One Act. By W. E. Suter. 4 Male, 3 Female characters.

15. **Done on Both Sides.** A Farce in One Act. By J. M. Morton. 3 Male, 2 Female characters.

16. **Dunducketty's Picnic.** A Farce in One Act. By T. J. Williams. 6 Male, 3 Female characters.

17. **I've written to Browne.** A Farce in One Act. By T. J. Williams. 4 Male, 3 Female characters.

18. **Lending a Hand.** A Farce in One Act. By G. A. A'Beckett. 3 Male, 2 Female characters.

19. **My Precious Betsy.** A Farce in One Act. By J. M. Morton. 4 Male, 4 Female characters.

20. **My Turn Next.** A Farce in One Act. By T. J. Williams. 4 Male, 3 Female characters.

21. **Nine Points of the Law.** A Comedy in One Act. By Tom Taylor. 4 Male, 3 Female characters.

22. **The Phantom Breakfast.** A Farce in One Act. By Charles Selby. 3 Male, 2 Female characters.

23. **Dandelions Dodges.** A Farce in One Act. By T. J. Williams. 4 Male, 2 Female characters.

24. **A Slice of Luck.** A Farce in One Act. By J. M. Morton. 4 Male, 2 Female characters.

25. **Always Intended.** A Comedy in One Act. By Horace Wigan. 3 Male, 3 Female characters.

26. **A Bull in a China Shop.** A Comedy in Two Acts. By Charles Matthews. 6 Male, 4 Female characters.

27. **Another Glass.** A Drama in One Act. By Thomas Morton. 6 Male, 3 Female characters.

28. **Bowled Out.** A Farce in One Act. By H. T. Craven. 4 Male, 3 Female characters.

29. **Cousin Tom.** A Commedietta in One Act. By George Roberts. 3 Male, 2 Female characters.

30. **Sarah's Young Man.** A Farce in One Act. By W. E. Suter. 3 Male, 3 Female characters.

31. **Hit Him, He has No Friends.** A Farce in One Act. By E. Yates and N. H. Harrington. 7 Male, 3 Female characters.

32. **The Christening.** A Farce in One Act. By J. B. Buckstone. 5 Male, 6 Female characters.

33. **A Race for a Widow.** A Farce in One Act. By Thomas J. Williams. 5 Male, 4 Female characters.

34. **Your Life's in Danger.** A Farce in One Act. By J. M. Morton. 3 Male, 3 Female characters.

35. **True unto Death.** A Drama in Two Acts. By J. Sheridan Knowles. 6 Male, 2 Female characters.

ABOVE THE CLOUDS.

BY THE AUTHOR OF

'Sylvia's Soldier,' "Once on a Time," "Down by the Sea," "Bread on the Waters," "The Last Loaf," "Stand by the Flag," "The Tempter," "A Drop Too Much," "We're All Teetotalers," "A Little More Cider," "Thirty Minutes for Refreshments," "Wanted, a Male Cook," "A Sea of Troubles," "Freedom of the Press," "A Close Shave," "The Great Elixir," "The Man with the Demijohn," "New Brooms Sweep Clean," "Humors of the Strike," "My Uncle the Captain," "The Greatest Plague in Life,' "No Cure, No Pay," "The Grecian Bend," "The War of the Roses," "Lightheart's Pilgrimage," "The Sculptor's Triumph," "Too Late for the Train," "Snow-Bound," "The Peddler of Very Nice," "Bonbons," "Capu-letta," "An Original Idea," "Enlisted for the War," "Never say Die," "The Champion of her Sex," "The Visions of Freedom," "The Merry Christ-mas of the Old Woman who lived in a Shoe," "The Tournament of Idylcourt, "A Thorn among the Roses," "A Christmas Carol," "One Hundred Years Ago," &c.

BOSTON:

GEORGE M. BAKER AND COMPANY,

41-45 FRANKLIN STREET.

Electrotyped at the Boston Stereotype Foundry,
19 Spring Lane.

ABOVE THE CLOUDS.

A DRAMA IN TWO ACTS.

CHARACTERS.

PHILIP RINGOLD, " Crazy Phil," a Mountain Hermit.
ALFRED THORPE, a City Nabob.
AMOS GAYLORD, a Country Gentleman.
HOWARD GAYLORD, his Son.
TITUS TURTLE, a Gourmand.
CURTIS CHIPMAN, " Chips" in the Rough.
NAT NAYLOR, Thorpe's Protegé.
GRACE INGALLS, a Young Artist.
HESTER THORNE, Gaylord's Housekeeper.
SUSY GAYLORD, Gaylord's Daughter.
LUCRETIA GERRISH, " so romantic."

COSTUMES.

RINGOLD. Age 40. Full black beard; thick, curly wig; slouch hat; long boots; light coat, buttoned at the waist; blue shirt, with black handkerchief knotted at the neck; collar of shirt rolled over coat.

ALFRED THORPE. Age 50. White, curly hair; white side-whiskers; fashionable dress; kids, and dress hat.

99

Amos Gaylord. Age 60. White wig; smooth face; nankeen vest and pants; blue coat with brass buttons; white tie.

Howard Gaylord. Age 24. First Dress: Dark cutaway coat; neat red shirt, with black neckerchief loosely .tied; dark pants, with leather leggings; wide-awake hat. — Second Dress: Neat and tasty suit.

Turtle. Age 40. Made up "fat"; fashionable fancy suit; red, curly hair; side-whiskers, and plump, red face.

Curtis. Age 20. Rough suit; pants, coat, and vest; light hat; light hair.

Nat. Age 20. First Dress: A light suit; green necktie; green gloves; straw hat, with a green ribbon. — Second Dress: Fashionable evening dress; white tie; dress coat; hair light, long, parted in the middle.

Grace. Age 18. First Dress: Pretty-figured muslin, or blue or brown cambric, fashionably cut. — Second Dress: White muslin.

Hester Thorne. Age 40. Brown or gray dress, with collar and cuffs; fine, white wig. Face made up young and rosy.

Susy. Age 17. First Dress: Figured muslin, with white apron; long ear-rings. Second Dress: Neat evening-dress.

Lucretia. Age 30. First Dress: Travelling-dress, as showy as possible; face made up wrinkled; very red cheeks; a profusion of red curls, and a black patch on left cheek. Second Dress: Light fabric, with ribbons and bows of scarlet.

STAGE DIRECTIONS.

R., right; c., centre; L., left; L. C., left centre; R. C., right centre; L. 1 E., left first entrance; R. 1 E., right first entrance; FLAT, scene at back of stage; R. U. E., right upper entrance.

ABOVE THE CLOUDS.

ACT I.—SCENE: *Room in* GAYLORD'S *house. In flat* C., *open doorway, backed by lattice-work, with vine running up it.* L. *of door, a long window, showing a railing backing it, and beyond that, shrubbery; the passage-way off is through door, then past window, and off* L. *Long curtains at window; a vase of flowers standing on the stage at back of open door; flat plain from door to* R. *with a picture hanging on it; long window* R. *next flat, with long curtain; lounge at window* R., *back to flat; small table at window* L. C., *with flowers and books upon it; chair front of it. Door* L. *half-way up stage; arm-chair* L. *Entrance* R. *Easel, with picture on it, back to audience, near window* R. GRACE *seated painting.* HOWARD *standing* C. *leaning on a gun, hat in hand, watching her.*

Grace. And you really like my picture, Mr. Gaylord?

Howard. Like it, Miss Grace? It's a bit of Nature filched from our grand old mountain so cleverly, that I wonder it does not give one of its thunder-growls in protest of the robbery.

Grace. It will be growled at by those monsters the art-critics. They will not spare a single tree, or a stone, in my Mountain-Picture. Ah, if they were only as kindly-disposed as you are, I should not fear.

Howard. Don't place me among them, Miss Grace. I'm but a rough-handed farmer, who would be laughed at in such company.

Grace. Yet you are an artist.

Howard. At ploughing — yes.

Grace. You may laugh; but you are a true artist. Yon wooded valley, stretching to the distant river; yon towering mountain, lifting its head above the clouds, thrill me with delight, as a holiday sight gladdens the heart of the child. But to you they are daily life. As the order, peace, and love of a household fill the heart of the child with all good impulses, so the clear mountain air you breathe, the majesty of Nature in its grand sublimity, train the eye to beauty, the soul to harmony, the heart to inspiration, — all unconscious influences which make you a critic whose praise is worth the winning.

Howard. You are enthusiastic.

Grace. Thank you. I am winning favor; for without enthusiasm how could we poor artists live?

Howard. Then you like our rough life here, far above the busy, bustling world?

Grace. Like it? To be free from the thraldom of city life, its crowded, bustling streets, its mockery of comfort, its greed and avarice, crime and folly, is to me as welcome, as joyous, as must be the sunlight to the prisoner for years confined in gloomy dungeons.

Howard. And you could forsake all that — could be happy here?

Grace. Forever.

Howard. O Grace,—Miss Ingalls,—you know not what pleasure that confession gives me. If I might hope —

(*Enter* Susy, *door* I.., *with a pan of apples and a knife.*)

Susy. O, I beg your pardon. Do I intrude?

Grace. No, indeed, Susy. I was just giving a few finishing touches to my picture, and Howard—Mr. Gaylord—was admiring the color of my sky.

Howard. Yes, Susy, that's all.

Susy. O! (*Aside*) Admiring the color! They've both got an extra quantity of red in their faces. (*Sits in arm-chair.*) The reflection of the picture, I suppose. (*Pares apples.*)

Grace. Are those hanging-clouds light enough?

Howard. Exactly the tints displayed at sunset. But to my mind, that quaint scene above the clouds is the beauty of the picture. Ringold's Nest, we call it — Crazy Phil's rocky hut.

Grace. The Hermit of the Mountain. I long to catch a glimpse of this mysterious hero of the Peak.

Howard. I am expecting him here every moment; but you must look at him outside, for he never enters a house. I go gunning with him to-day.

Grace. Gunning with a crazy man?

Howard. Phil is not crazy. His eccentricities have gained him that title here. Ten years ago he passed through here to the Peak, and took possession of the rude hut upon its summit. A wan, ragged, and haggard man. Occasionally he comes into our streets, but shuns our abodes. His mountain life has made a new man of him; improved his health and spirits; and I want no better companion on a tramp, no wiser friend in council, than Phil Ringold.

Grace. And his past history?

Howard. Is a sealed book. Occasionally, in fits of abstraction, he mutters hoarsely of a faithless wife, a lost child, a false friend; but when I question him, he is silent.

Grace. Brave fellow! Foiled in his battle with the world, he turns his back upon it, and in Nature's solitudes fashions a new life and battles with himself.

Howard. One would imagine, from your poor opinion of the world you have left, that even you — young, talented, and — well, it is the truth — beautiful, had met with disappointment.

Grace. No; I have nothing to complain of, except the fact that I am nobody is a disappointment.

Howard. Nobody! You — you have genius.

Grace. Perhaps. That remains to be seen. I know I have courage to persevere, will to conquer; but, should I triumph, none to rejoice at my success.

Howard. I do not understand you.

Grace. Because you do not know me. I do not know myself. I am a waif, the property of nobody who will claim me. Originally, one of those mysterious little mortals that are dropped by the way, as we sometimes dispose of a troublesome kitten.

Howard. And your parents?

Grace. I have not the honor of their acquaintance; nothing but the recollection of a loving face bending over me; a silken beard I loved to stroke, long, long years ago; and then a change to rough hands, but kind hearts; and then all is blotted, till my life began with Mr. Thorpe.

Howard. Surely that was a pleasant change.

Grace. He says he was a friend of my parents; that both are dead — and nothing more. Where they lived, or where they lie, in vain I ask. He has ever been a kind friend to me; allowed me to choose my artist life; spared no expense; encouraged me in every way; and yet, and yet — I hate him!

Howard. Hate him?

Grace. What right has he to stand between me and those who gave me life?

Howard. But if they are dead?

Grace (rising). Their memories should live in the heart of their child; not be stolen from her; hidden away in the grave with them, as though they were guilty things, too base to be remembered. No, no; there is some mystery here. Would I could solve it *(raises hand towards window R. and looks off).* O, solitary dweller on the Mountain Peak, I can clasp hands with thee. Thou standest alone in Nature's loneliest haunts; amid the crowded ways of life, like thee, I am alone — alone. *(With an effort.)* Pardon me; this is one of my changeful moods. I shall soon be better. [*Exit* R. 1 E.

Howard. A strange mood. So young; so beautiful. She fascinates me! Am I wise to linger in her presence? To listen to her beguiling voice? To look into her eyes? · She, a genius, and an angel! Dare I utter the words that spring to my lips —

Susy. Ahem!

Howard. Susy, I had forgotten you. What are you doing, puss?

Susy. O, I've been keeping Miss Grace and you company.

Howard. In what way?

Susy. Paring! O, Howard Gaylord, you've just come, and been and gone and done it.

Howard. What, puss?

Susy. Fallen in love with Miss Grace Ingalls.

Howard. Nonsense, puss.

Susy. Well, I think there is a great deal of non-sense about it. But ain't it nice to feel your heart going pitity-pat, pitity-pat, every time she looks at you, and to feel that delicious lump in your throat, like as though you were going to strangle with delight and was afraid you shouldn't!

Howard. Well, you certainly understand the symp-toms, Susy.

Susy. Indeed I do. I haven't lived seventeen years for nothing. But all that's nothing to what will come over you the first time you clasp her taper fin-gers. You'll feel just as though you were being lifted upon a bridge of rainbows. You'll be dizzy at first, but it soon wears off.

Howard. Ha, ha! you're well posted, puss. Was Curtis Chipman your instructor?

Susy. Chips? Not much; he hasn't the courage to look me in the eye.

Howard. And of course cannot feel the " pitity-pat " sensation. Curt is a good fellow, Susy; mind you don't frighten him.

Susy. I frighten him! He don't need any help, he frightens himself.

Howard. And you think I love Miss Grace?

Susy. You prove it, in being so anxious to return to the subject.

Howard. What if I do, Susy. Do you think she would condescend to look with favor upon such a rough specimen as I?

Susy. Condescend? My goodness! Condescend to you, my brother? The idea! Why, Howard Gaylord, I'm ashamed of you! You're none *too good* for the best woman that ever trod the earth.

Howard. Ha, ha, ha! Right, Susy: I'm none " too good."

Susy. Now laugh because I made a slip. You know what I mean; and if you don't boldly woo and win Grace Ingalls, I'll disinherit you.

Howard. Hush! she's here.

Susy. I thought she couldn't keep away from you long.

(*Enter* GRACE, R.)

Grace. There, the storm is over (*goes to her easel*).

Susy (*aside*). Now's the time for rainbows! Why don't he squeeze her hand?

Howard. Shall I disturb you if I look at your work?

Grace. O, no; I'm quite myself again.

Susy (*aside*). Look at her work, indeed! He can't keep his eyes off of her. (*Whistle outside*, L. SUSY *gradually falls asleep.*)

Howard. Ah, that's Phil Ringold. I must be off.

Grace. O, do bring him in.

Howard. I cannot; it would be useless to make the attempt.

Grace (*rising*). Then I'll have one good look at him (*rises and goes up into doorway; looks off* L.). Yes, what a fine figure. Mr. Gaylord, your friend is splendid. Ah, he sees me (*bows and smiles*). He starts. He comes this way like a madman (*runs down to easel; turns and stands with hand on easel, bending forward, looking at door.* HOWARD, L.)

Phil (*outside,* L.). Hester! Hester! (*Passes window and appears in doorway, gun thrown across his arm; stops and glares at* GRACE.) Hester! No, no; 'tis her face; but she — so like! so like! Where got you that face? It belonged to one I knew long years ago. So beautiful — but false. As young and fair, but heartless and cruel. She made my home a ruin and my life a curse.

Howard. Phil, old fellow, be calm. This is our guest, Miss Grace Ingalls — an artist. Look at her work there on the easel. Do you recognize it? (GRACE *steps back towards window,* R. PHIL *comes forward, his eyes fastened upon her face until he nears the easel. He sighs; lets his eyes rove round until they reach the picture; starts.*)

Phil (*with a smile*). Ah, the old nest. See, see, Howard! It's wondrous like — wondrous like! (*Turns to* GRACE *with a bow.*) I congratulate you, young lady, on your success. It is a charming picture.

Grace. Thank you.

Phil (*starts*). O, that voice! — it brings back the old days — the mother with the child in her lap; and

the music of her lullaby thrills me again and again.
No, no; let me shut it out — shut it out; it softens
my heart, — and that should be steel, adamant, to bar
out forever the traitoress, the false one. Come, Howard, the day is speeding, and we've a long tramp. Come,
come (*goes up*).

Grace. Stay one moment. (PHIL *turns.*) We meet
as strangers to-day; but, believe me, I sympathize with
your sorrows and your wrongs. Can we not be friends?
(*Offers her hand.*)

Phil (*takes it and looks in her face*). My sorrows
and my wrongs, child, they are forgotten. I trod
the haunts of men, mingled with the bustling and the
busy; loved, lost; and then, there (*pointing off through
window, R.*) on yonder mountain peak, perched myself
above the clouds, that, floating at my feet, shut out all
tokens of the sin and wrong below. Ah, little one,
pretty one, this is a world of trouble. We joy and
we sorrow, gain and lose; but there — there on His
eternal mountains that pierce the sky, all is forgotten,
for we are alone, — with Nature here, and Heaven
there.

Grace. May Heaven recompense you for all you
have suffered.

Phil. It will; it does. My wrongs were like those
of other men. I loved, and was deceived. I married,
and found my wife's smiles were bestowed upon another. I was a fool to trust a woman, and so pay pen-
ance by forgetting the whole world.

Howard. Except —

Phil (*giving* HOWARD *his hand*). Except Howard,

for we are friends, and he is of my own mind. He'll never trust a woman. (Howard *withdraws his hand, looks at* Grace, *and turns away.* Grace *blushes and looks down.*) Ho, ho! I've said too much. Never mind; it's only Crazy Phil. Come, Howard, we must be off, for game's afoot, and Crazy Phil is a wondrous good shot. Ha, ha, ha! (*At door, turns and bows to* Grace.) Good-bye. So like — so like — it almost drives me mad.   [*Exit* c. *off* l.

Howard. You see, Miss Grace, Phil is an odd character.

Grace. Very.

Howard. You mustn't mind all he says; for instance, that remark about me that I would never trust a woman; for there is one woman I could trust with my life, my soul.

Grace. I hope there are many such.

Howard. Yes — O, yes. But this one —

Grace. Your friend is waiting, I see.

Howard. I'm off. (*Aside*) She's not for me — not for me. I was a fool to think it.   [*Bows, and exit* c.

Grace. I'm on dangerous ground here. This rough but honest-hearted fellow is stirring my heart strangely. Is fate or fortune about to send some one to prove false my statement that there's no one to rejoice at my success? If so, I hope he'll be the man. [*Exit* r. 1 e.

(*Enter* Chips *from* l. *He comes on with his hat twirling in his hand; comes to door slowly and stands looking down bashfully, rubbing against door-post.*)

Chips. I was just going by. (*Pause*). I said I was

just going by (*looks up*). Hallo! Nobody here? That's queer, I vum! (*Comes down.*) I've made up my mind that Susy Gaylord is the prettiest, smartest, and likeliest gal in these parts, and I've just got spunk enough to tell her so. (*Sees* SUSY.) Jewhittiker! there she is! (*Backs across stage to* R., *looking down and twirling his hat.*) How d'e do? I was just going by. (*Pause, looks up.*) Why, she's asleep! (*Comes to c. and looks at her.*) Now, ain't she a beauty! just clear pink and white. Look at them lips! there 's honey for the taking! Curtis, now's your chance (*wipes his mouth with coat-sleeve*). She 's asleep, and nobody 's looking (*creeps towards her*).

(*Enter* NAT NAYLOR, L.; *looks through window.*) I'm trembling all over ; but, darn it, here goes! (*Stoops to kiss her.* NAT *comes to door.*)

Nat. Brace up! (CHIPS *runs across stage to* R. SUSY *wakes.* NAT *comes down.*) Here 's robbery! Grand larceny!

> Bumpkin, forbear, touch not those tempting lips,
> Base is the man who thus felonious sips.

Impromptu. Ahem! (*To* SUSY) Excuse me, I am the *avant courier* of Mr. Alfred Thorpe, Mr. Titus Turtle, " and last but not least is our dear love," Miss Lucretia Gerrish, — three mountain travellers who are on their way to spend a few days in this delightful mansion of Mr. Amos Gaylord.

> A stately pile, the country's pride and boast,
> Amid the mountain, with *A Gaylord* host.

Impromptu. Ahem! (*Struts up stage.*)

Susy. Well, I never!

Chips. Wall, he's gone crazy, and got it bad.

Susy. Chips, what are you doing here?

Nat (comes down). Chips, is it? O, Chips, I blush for you. Young lady, look upon me as your preserver. I caught this modest rustic in the very act of snatching a kiss from those ruby lips, —

> Where Cupid sits enthroned with arching bow,
> Before the ivoried walls that gleam below.

Impromptu. Ahem!

Susy. Chips, is it possible? Did you dare?

Chips. Well, you see, Susy, I was going by, and — and — I thought I'd just drop in to tell you that — that — mother's making pickles to-day.

Nat. O, Chips! Chips!

> While making pickles, mother dear,
> I find a sweeter pickle here.

Impromptu. Ahem!

Chips. Look here, Mr. What's-your-name, you're a darned sight too free with your Mother Goose Melodies. Ef you get my dander up, you'll think a horse kicked you, — now I tell you.

Susy. Chips, don't be rude.

Chips. Well, I ain't a-goin' to be sassed by a feller that can't talk English.

Nat. Chips, you want polish.

Chips. Well, p'raps you'd like to polish me. Ef you would, I'm your man. Come down behind the barn —

Susy. Chips, I'm ashamed of you!

Nat. So am I, Chips.

> The blush of shame is mounting to my cheek,
> It glows —

It glows — There, I've lost it! You must know, I'm a *protégé* of Mr. Thorpe's, destined to become a poet. Yes, he's fond of helping aspiring genius up the dizzy heights — and I'm to be a poet. So, as practice makes perfect, I indulge in flights of fancy on all occasions. So if you happen to hear from my lips eccentric bits, don't mind them. It's nothing — mere practice.

Susy. O, you're a poet! Well, I declare!

Nat. Yes — Nat Naylor. Sometimes called Natty, because my verses are neat and natty. See?

Susy. I am glad to welcome you to my father's house.

Nat. Then I am in the presence of Miss Susy Gaylord. Delighted to make your acquaintance. Allow me — (*lifts her hand to his lips*).

> Here on this hand I pay the homage due
> To lovely woman —

(*About to kiss again*)

Susy (*withdrawing her hand*). Thank you; that will do.

Nat. Impromptu. Ahem! I must return to my friends. You may expect us in half an hour. Adieu (*goes to door and turns*). We part to meet again.— Sweet one, farewell. Chips, *au revoir.* [*Exit* c.

Chips. Get out, you tarnal swell! Darn his picture, I'll have one shot at him. (*Runs up to* Susy, *takes three or four apples, and runs up to* c.)

8

Susy.   Chips, what are you doing with my apples?

Chips (throwing apples off L. *swiftly).*   There, impromptu!   Darn you!   I wish they were Centennial eggs!   (*Comes down* C.)

Susy.   Curtis Chipman!

Chips.   That's my name, and I ain't ashamed of it.

Susy.   I'm ashamed of you!   Such treatment of a gentleman and a poet!

Chips.   O, bother!   What's a poet, anyhow?   He can't tell a Shanghai from a Bantam, a pitchfork from a rake.   What right has he to kiss your hand?   You never saw me trying it?

Susy.   No; but he saw you attempting something worse, Chips.

Chips.   Don't care.   I was just going by —

Susy.   Pshaw!   you're always going by.   Why don't you come straight to the house, and not make an excuse, when you know you are dying to see me.   O, Chips, you're a good fellow, but you want a little polish.   Look at Mr. Naylor.

Chips.   Hang Mr. Naylor!   I hate him.

Susy.   And I like him.   He's so gentle, so well-bred; such a flow of language.   I'm sure we shall become good friends.

Chips (throws his hat on stage).   Susy Gaylord, I'm mad; and I'm going to tell you just what I think of you.

Susy.   That's right, Chips; frankness is a virtue.

Chips.   You're a — a — confound it, Susy, you're an angel; and I love you better than father or mother, sister or brother —

Susy. Uncles and aunts, first and second cousins. Put in all the relatives, Chips.

Chips. I know I ain't handsome.

Susy. So do I, Chips.

Chips. I haven't what you call "polish."

Susy. Not a bit, Chips.

Chips. But I've got a heart crammed full of love for you. Will you marry me?

Susy. I cannot, Chips; because — because —

Chips. Because what?

Susy. I'm an angel; and angels don't marry.

Chips. Don't torture me, Susy.

Susy. No, Chips — I should if I married you. So I'll be merciful and spare you.

> An angel of mercy, hovering nigh,
> To watch your footsteps when you're going by.

Impromptu. Ahem!

Chips. Hang it! don't you go to making melodies and jingles — Naylor's lingo. All fools make rhymes; they do, by jingo!

Susy. Impromptu. Ahem! Ha, ha, ha!

Chips. You won't have me?

Susy. Haven't got time. Strangers are coming here, you know, and I must be bustling. All of them coming, including that delightful Mr. Naylor.

Chips. Darn him! You'll be sorry for this, Susy Gaylord. As for that poet fellow, if I don't smash his rhyming-machine, then my name 's not Curtis Chipman (*goes off* c.).

Susy. Good-bye, Chips; call again when you 're

going by.   Ha, ha, ha!   I've found a new way to make
a bashful lover speak.   Get him mad, and then he dis-
closes his passion.   Ha, ha, ha!   (*Goes up and puts pan
of apples on table.*)

(*Enter* AMOS GAYLORD, C.)

Amos.   Susy, has Mrs. Thorne returned?

Susy.   No, father; she spent the night at Mrs.
Green's, with her sick boy.

Amos.   Bless her! that woman's a sister of charity,
Susy; a friend in trouble; the poor pray for her, and
the sick forget their pain when she is near.

Susy.   Ah, father, you've a tender regard for our
new housekeeper.

Amos.   To be sure I have, Susy.   Isn't she a treasure here?   How carefully she looks after my comfort;
so quiet, yet so active at her household duties; so un-
obtrusive; so motherly to you.   Ah, it was a happy
day when she came to our home!

Susy.   Father, you surprise me!

Amos.   I have a still greater surprise in store for
you, Susy.   I am going to ask Mrs. Thorne to marry
me.

Susy.   Marry you!

Amos.   Yes; she has become so necessary here that
I fear to lose her.   She has evidently seen trouble,
poverty.   Why should not I try to make her forget all
she has suffered by making her the honored head of
this my home?

Susy.   Father, no one would more gladly welcome
her to that position than I.   I truly, sincerely hope

you may be successful; but I fear you will be disappointed.

Amos. Don't dash my hopes, Susy! I'm not a very old man. I have wealth.

Susy. Any woman might be proud of your proposal, father; but she has that in her face which tells me she has suffered deeply.

Hester (*outside* c.). I will have it attended to at once.

Amos. Hush! she is here.

(*Enter* HESTER THORNE *from* L., *passing window to* c. *door. She has a light shawl on her shoulders, a rigolette on her head.*)

Hester. Good morning, Mr. Gaylord. Susy, have you missed me?

Susy. We always miss you, Mrs. Thorne. (*Takes her shawl and rigolette.*) How is the boy?

Hester. Poor little fellow! — at rest; he died this morning. Brave to the last, he suffered uncomplainingly, and passed away with a smile upon his lips.

Amos. You have had a weary night. You must take rest. (*Exit* SUSY, *door* L.)

Hester. No; my brisk walk this morning has refreshed me.

Amos. I do not like to have you waste your strength in such constant watching.

Hester. I think one gains strength in seeking to alleviate distress.

Amos. Yes; but —

Hester. You think it unfits me for my duties as your housekeeper.

Amos. Mrs. Thorne!

Hester. Pardon me; that was an unkind speech to so generous a man as you.

Amos. I think only of your own health, Mrs. Thorne. I am anxious on your account solely. For a year you have been my housekeeper, and I need not tell you how highly you are respected here.

Hester. I am glad to know you like me.

Amos. So well, Mrs. Thorne, that I am anxious to secure you for life.

Hester (*surprised*). Mr. Gaylord!

Amos. Hester Thorne, I am too old a man to prate of love with a young man's passionate warmth. I have the most exalted opinion of your disposition, your talents, and your honor. Will you become my wife?

Hester. Mr. Gaylord, you know not what you ask. Impossible!

Amos. Impossible! Mrs. Thorne, I am a man of few words; but I am honest, earnest in my offer. Give your consent, and you are mistress here.

Hester. Stop — stop — give me time —

Amos. To consider my proposal?

Hester. No, no; not that. It must not, cannot be. O, you have taken me by surprise. I never dreamed of this. Your offer is generous, noble. You have been a kind, dear friend to me, and I respect you; but marriage! — No, no — there is a bar.

Amos. You are a widow?

Hester. Widow or wife, Heaven alone can answer. Mr. Gaylord, there must be no secrets between us now. Listen to me; listen to a story never breathed to mortal ears before. Years ago, I, a young girl, was wooed by two suitors, both handsome and accomplished. One became my partner, and, for a year, happiness was my lot.   Then a child was born to me, and still my happiness continued ; my husband loved me, and my home was heaven itself. When our little girl was three years old, the other suitor returned from a foreign land. My husband and he were intimate ; he came to our house, and in an evil hour professed his love for me. I spurned him ; but still he came. Then I committed the first error of my married life. I kept his secret from my husband, but still avoided him with loathing and abhorrence. He — villain that he was — filled his friend's ears with slanderous reports. My husband grew cold, and still my lips were closed. One night — shall I ever forget it ? — I awoke to find myself alone. My husband had fled with our child, leaving behind, in letters that burned into my brain, his bitter taunts for my unfaithfulness and guilt. O, heavens, I, innocent and loving, to be so accused ! From that day I have never seen them.

Amos. But could you find no clue ?

Hester. None ; day followed day, and still I waited. A year passed, and I read in a paper, marked for my inspection, the death of my child in a distant city.

Amos. Was no provision made for your support?

Hester. Ample ; but I was too proud to take his wealth while he believed me guilty. With my own hands I toiled, patiently trusting to time to work out the right. Years have followed years, and still I wait. O Heaven, be merciful ; shed some light upon my dark path, ere I go down into the grave. Let him believe me innocent, and death will be a welcome release.

Amo . This is a sad story, Mrs. Thorne. I thank you for the telling. You have a friend in me, trust me — a home here among us. You have been deeply wronged, and I'll search the world over, but your innocence shall be made clear.

Hester. No, no; let it rest. Were my child living, for her sake I would be vindicated; but I am alone, and, confident in my own integrity, can wait the righteous verdict in the great hereafter. [*Exit door* L.

Amos. She's a noble woman; there's goodness and honesty in her face. 'Tis hard to lose her; but I'll have the truth, wherever it rests.

(*Enter* ALFRED THORPE, C.)

Thorpe. Ah, my old friend, your doors are open, and, of course, the latch-string is out.

Amos (*shaking hands*). Thorpe, welcome, welcome; this is a surprise.

Thorpe. Indeed! Then my poetical *protégé*, Nat Naylor, has surely not performed his duty. I sent him here to announce my coming.

Amos. No matter; it needed no ceremony; we are always ready to receive you.

Thorpe. And my friends, I trust. But where's my Grace, and how is she? Enraptured with your delightful scenery, I'll be bound.

Amos. Yes; enjoying herself hugely. She's a genius, Thorpe. Where did you find such a treasure?

Thorpe. Ah, that's a secret. But, between you and

me, she's the daughter of a couple whose married life
was not as happy as it should have been. The wife
went astray, and the husband went roaming, nobody
knows where.

Amos. And Grace — does she know of this?

Thorpe. No; she believes them both dead.

Amos. Ah, and their names?

Thorpe. O come, come, old friend, you are getting
excited. I've told you quite enough. The rest is my
secret. The intrigues of the world in which I live can
scarcely interest you in your simple, honest, country life.

Amos. And you are content to practise this decep-
tion upon a young girl?

Thorpe. Who would be made unhappy by the
knowledge I withhold? Yes, believe me, old friend, in
all I do, I am anxious to secure her happiness; for she
has become very dear to me — so dear that I am here
for the sole purpose of asking her to become my wife.

Amos. Ah, this is a part of your secret?

Thorpe. Yes. I've told you I am a man of the
world. I never allow anything to thwart me in my
inclinations and desires. She is dependent upon me.
I have made her young life pleasant and happy. Every
wish has been gratified, every desire fulfilled. She
looks upon me as her benefactor; and when I ask her
hand, I have no fear of a refusal.

Amos. But there's such a difference in your ages.
She may respect you as her benefactor, but when you
ask her love, she may rebel.

Thorpe. Possibly; but when she hears the story of
her parents — when she knows that by making it pub-

lic she might feel the stigma of their shame, she'll be glad to buy my silence.

Amos. And you could do this?

Thorpe. Certainly, if by no other means I could gain her consent.

Amos. Why, this is cowardly, unmanly. Thorpe, I would not believe you could be guilty of so base a deed.

Thorpe. Tut, tut; this is the way of the world — my world.

Amos. Then your world is a province of the infernal kingdom!

Thorpe. Possibly. And yours, of the better world; for here you are much nearer to the heavens. Come, come, old friend, keep my secret and lead me to my *protégé*.

Amos. She's here. (*Goes up stage.*)

(*Enter* GRACE, R.)

Thorpe. Ah, Grace! Grace!

Grace (*running to him and taking his hand*). Welcome, a thousand times welcome, Mr. Thorpe!

Thorpe. What a change! The mountain air has put a rich color in your face; you are wondrous beautiful, child. So you are glad to meet me again?

Grace. Indeed — indeed I am. If the mountain air has freshened my complexion, my absence from you has freshened the recollection of how much I owe to you, — how grateful I should be for all your care of me.

Turtle (*outside* c.). How soon will dinner be ready?

Thorpe. Ah, there's Turtle; with characteristic instinct he is sniffing the country air to catch a whiff from the kitchen fire. (*Goes up* c.) This way, Turtle. (AMOS *comes to* R. *and speaks with* GRACE.)

Turtle (*outside* c.). It's very well to say this way; but, considering what I weigh, you'd better let me have my way in getting up. (*Passes window with* LUCRETIA *on his arm, and enters* c.) Thorpe, this is a wretched country; it's all up stairs.

Thorpe. Don't grumble, old fellow. Mr. Gaylord, my friend Titus Turtle.

Amos. Glad to see you (*shakes hands*).

Turtle. Thank you. Fine place you have, Mr. Gaylord. Ah, my little friend Grace! (*Passes* AMOS, *and takes her hand.*) And how are you? Hearty, eh?

Grace. Quite well, thank you, and delighted to meet you again.

Thorpe. (*To* AMOS, *presenting* MISS GERRISH.) My friend, Miss Gerrish.

Amos. Happy to meet you, and hope to make your stay pleasant in our homely way.

Lucretia. Thank you. 'Tis really a delightful place; delightful trees; delightful hills; delightful odors; and all — so romantic.

Turtle. Right, Miss Lucretia (*snuffs*); delightful odor (*snuffs*). (*Aside*) Roast mutton.

Lucretia (*running to window,* R.). O, Mr. Turtle, do come here, quick; such an exquisite prospect!

Turtle (*goes to table*). Thank you; here's a finer prospect to my taste (*takes apple and eats*).

Lucretia. How gracefully those boughs bend towards the ground.

Turtle. They can't help it; they're loaded down with apples.

Lucretia. And do see those lambs frolicking in the sunshine. Sportive, innocent creatures. I do love lambs — so romantic.

Turtle (*helping himself to another apple*). So do I — with mint-sauce.

Lucretia. And do see that poor dumb animal fastened there in the grass, like a martyr at the stake.

Turtle. Ah, what luscious steaks he 'll make when he 's cut up! Mr. Gaylord, what is the dinner hour in this mountainous country?

Amos. Twelve o'clock, Mr. Turtle.

Turtle (*looking at watch*). O! — two hours, thirty-five minutes and ten seconds (*sinks into arm-chair*, L.). I shall starve before that time!

Amos. Suppose we furnish you a lunch?

Turtle. Capital idea, Mr. Gaylord; I've not eaten anything since six o'clock!

Thorpe. Titus!

Lucretia. Mr. Turtle!

Turtle. Well, nothing worth mentioning.

Thorpe. The lunch-basket was very heavy when we started. It is empty now; and neither Miss Gerrish nor I have helped unload it. If I recollect right, there were a pair of chickens.

Turtle. Only six pounds! What's that to a hungry man?

Lucretia. Three dozen sandwiches.

Turtle. Mere wafers!

Thorpe. Two dozen eggs.

Turtle. So very small!

Thorpe. A box of sardines; two dozen crackers; and turnovers enough to stock a country muster. O, Turtle, you cannot be hungry after such a feast.

Turtle. Feast? Call that a feast? Thorpe, I blush for you! You're getting niggardly! I shall have to be caterer for the balance of our trip.

Thorpe. Then I'll provide a baggage-wagon.

Lucretia. O, Mr. Turtle — dear Mr. Turtle, do make me happy by leading me to those flower-beds that bloom outside the window?

Thorpe. Yes, Turtle; and Grace and I will bear you company.

Turtle. That's right, Thorpe. You take them both, and I'll join you after I've had my lunch.

Grace. I'll show the way. Come. [*Exit* R. 1 E.

(LUCRETIA *takes* THORPE'S *arm.*)

Thorpe (*aside*). Confound that glutton, he's spoiled a fine *tête-à-tête* with Grace. (*Aloud*) Turtle, remember where you are, and don't make a hog of yourself.

[*Exeunt* THORPE *and* LUCRETIA, R. 1 E.

Turtle. Now that's unkind of Thorpe. Is there anything about me, Mr. Gaylord, that bears the least resemblance to a hog? Hogs don't go upon two legs. Hogs have no delicate appreciation of the delights of eating. Hog indeed!

Amos. Never mind, Mr. Turtle; it's one of Thorpe's pleasantries.

Turtle. But I don't like it; it's a rude attack upon the fundamental principles of my being. Nature endowed me with uncommonly fine digestive faculties and gastronomic talents. I didn't ask Nature to do it; but having received what I did receive, it is my duty to use my talents — isn't it?

Amos. Undoubtedly, Mr. Turtle.

Turtle. Thorpe has no taste. He 's all head; forever scheming. Smart, but unscrupulous. For proof — years ago we both enjoyed the hospitalities of a friend. Such dinners! my mouth waters at the thought. I made love to our friend's table; he to our friend's wife; consequence was — while I only broke bread, he broke up the family. Well, of the two, I'd rather be a hog than a serpent, for hogs are death on snakes.

Amos (*aside*) Ah, this is news indeed!

Turtle. Then there's the girl Grace Ingalls. There's a queer story there. When he took her from old Jack Graham's house, at Greenland, she passed by another name than that. Hog indeed! A hog would have to root long and well to unearth the secret you have kept so well, Alfred Thorpe.

Amos. Ah, the secret!

Turtle. Eh? O, bah! that's my nonsense, Mr. Gaylord; don't mind it. Come, let 's to lunch.

Amos (*aside*) Ah, he's crawled into his shell again —this Turtle. But enough; I have a clue. (*Aloud*) Be patient, Mr. Turtle, I will have it arranged at once.

[*Exit door* L.

Turtle. The old fellow looks hearty, and I've no doubt has a good larder.

(*Enter* Naylor, c.)

Nat. Ah, Turtle, my boy, I've been looking for you.

Give me my turtle — crying everywhere,
Until the echoes sent mock-turtle through the air.

Impromptu. Ahem!

Turtle. Now don't do that, Nat; you'll spoil my appetite. Those spasms of wit must be an awful strain on your weak brain. Rhyming is a sure sign of dyspepsia; but when to that you add punning, you are digging a pit that will undermine your constitution.

Nat. What matters this frail structure unto me?
I feed upon the heights of Poesy.

Turtle. Must be high old feeding, — if you're a specimen, Nat.

Nat. I hear afar the sound of rippling rills;
I scent the verdure of a thousand hills.

Turtle. No, you don't. (*Snuffs.*) That's mutton roasting. (*Snuffs.*) Glorious — isn't it? O, will dinner-time never come?

(*Enter* SUSY, *door* L.)

Susy. Lunch is on the table, sir.

Turtle. Ah, that's glorious news! Come, Nat, join me with a knife and fork. I'll show you poetry — the poetry of motion from the hand to the mouth — something you can feel; something you can taste. Come on. [*Exit* L.

Susy. Will you follow him, Mr. Naylor?

Nat. While such an angel hovers in my way?
Thank you; at present, think I'd rather stay.

Impromptu. Ahem!

Susy. That's very pretty. Going to stay long?

Nat. Well, Miss Susy, I cannot say. It seems to me I have been here too long already.

> My fluttering heart in piteous accents cries,
> Naylor, begone; for here sweet danger lies.

Impromptu. Ahem!

Susy. O, there's nothing here to hurt you; a few snakes and woodchucks. Ain't afraid of woodchucks, are you?

Nat. • Were they as fierce as lions, I would rout,

> Yea, from your presence I *would chuck* them out.

Impromptu. Ahem! •

Susy. O what a man for rhyming! Do you know, Mr. Naylor, I am something of a poet?

Nat. You? Charming! I felt there was some hidden beauty about you which attracted me.

Susy. O yes; I make verses — (*aside*) as ridiculous as yours. You'll find them all over the house. There's a sweet little legend of mine over the back door: —

> Stranger pilgrim, pause awhile;
> On this door-step, broad and flat,
> Let no stains of earth defile;
> Wipe your boots upon the mat.

(*Aside*) Impromptu. Ahem!

Nat. Splendid! Beautiful! The true poetic principle.

Susy. Think so? Well, here's another. Mine are domestic verses.

> Wanderer, at the dizzy brink
> Of this freshly-painted sink,
> Beware the thrifty housewife's grow(e)l;
> On its peg hang up the towel.

(*Aside*) Impromptu. Ahem!

Nat. Exquisite! So appropriate! Ah, Miss Susy, I toil over an humble rhyme in the hope that one of these days I shall strike a mine of poetic metal that shall make the world ring with the music of my verse. Now, that's a pretty sentiment, if I could only put it into verse.

Susy. Perhaps I could help you.

Nat. O, if you only would, I should adore you.

Susy. Would you? Suppose we wander in the garden — there's so much there to inspire?

Nat. With pleasure. (*Offers his arm.*)

Susy (*taking it.*) You want to strike a mine?

Nat. I aim to reach a rich poetic mine.

Susy. As green and sappy as a towering pine. How's that?

Nat. Very bad, Miss Susy. Pines have nothing in common with mines.

Susy. Certainly they do. Ain't they both blasted? Well, if you don't like that, try again.

Nat. Grant me to find the true poetic mine,

Susy. That laurels may my burning brow entwine.

Nat. O, that's capital! I'd be the poorest scholar in thy school.

Susy. Stood on a bench, and plainly labelled — fool! Ha, ha, ha! Impromptu. Ahem! (*Runs off c.*) Ha, ha, ha!

Nat (*following*). Now Miss Susy! how could you?
[*Exit* c.

(*Enter* GRACE, R. 1 E.)

Grace. There's something in Mr. Thorpe's manner I do not like. Twice he has seized my hand with a

9

fervor that startled me; and continually his eyes are fixed upon my face with a look that terrifies me (*goes to easel*). So I've left him to listen to Miss Gerrish's rhapsodies. Ha, ha, ha! So romantic (*works at her picture*).

(*Enter* HESTER, *door* L..)

Hester. Good morning, Grace (*comes to easel*).

Grace (*extending her hand*). Good morning, dear friend. We have missed you sadly.

Hester. Indeed! 'Tis pleasant to be missed. And how comes on our famous picture?

Grace. Judge for yourself.

Hester (*looking at picture*). Ah, better and better. It improves with every touch of your brush (*lays hand on her head*). Ah, my dear, you will become famous!

Grace. And that is something to be desired.

Hester. Yes; when laurels can be worn modestly, as you will wear them (*removes her hand*).

Grace. Don't take your hand away; its caress symbolizes something to be desired more than laurels.

Hester (*replacing her hand*). And that is —

Grace. Affection. O, Mrs. Thorne, a mother's touch could be no more gentle and soothing — and that I have not felt for years.

Hester (*kisses her*). Poor child!

Grace. O, thank you, Mrs. Thorne; you are a mother?

Hester. Alas! a childless mother. Once I clasped a tiny form, showered kisses on its infant lips, stroked with tenderness its golden locks, and was so happy. But we were parted; and the sweet memory of that happy union are all that's left me now. O, my little daughter! my darling, darling child! (*Weeps.*)

Grace. (*Rises and puts her arm about her waist; leads her down front.*) O, would I could take that daughter's place; not to drive her from your heart, but to share with her its love — the living and the dead!

Hester. O, Grace, there's a tone in your voice, a look on your face, that brings her back to me. Had she lived, she would have been of your age.

Grace. Then let her live in me. I could toil for you, suffer for you, to be recompensed with the delight of calling you "mother."

Hester. Then call me — No, no; I had forgotten. Grace, that name cannot be given me now. My fair fame has been tampered with. O Grace, child, pity me. I am innocent in thought and deed, but the sharp dart of suspicion has been launched at me, and I must bear the sting.

Grace. But not alone. Let me share your sorrow; comfort you as you can comfort me.

Hester. No, no, it cannot be. I should love you so dearly, that when the sneers of the world should come — as come they would — and should part us, my misery would be more than I could bear. Heaven help me, I am indeed accursed! (*Totters to arm-chair, throws herself into it; covers her face with her handkerchief, and weeps.*)

Grace, c. O, this is cruel!

Thorpe (*outside* c.). Grace, Grace! (*Enters* c. *and comes down* R.) You little witch, why do you run away from me, when I've come here on purpose to see you? (*Takes her hand.*) Yes, Grace, to woo you?

Grace. To woo — me? (HESTER *removes her hand-kerchief, and stares at him.*)

Thorpe. Yes, Grace; you shall be my wife: I love you so dearly.

Grace. No, no, not that. (*Snatches away her hand, and runs* R., *leaving him staring at* HESTER.) Death rather.   [*Exit* R. 1 E.

Thorpe (*amazed*). Hester Thorne!

Hester (*bending forward*). Ay, Alfred Thorpe, Hester Thorne, the woman you have wronged. Coward! Twelve years have not changed your heart, though your locks have all the beauty of honorable years. (*Rises.*)

Thorpe. Well, we meet again. How? as friends or foes?

Hester. Can you ask? Dare you ask? You, who with smooth tongue and smiling face blasted a happy home, wrecked a good man's happiness, and sent a loving woman forth to battle with the world.

Thorpe. Hm! Well, I have your answer — Foes. So be it. What are you doing here?

Hester. My duty.

Thorpe. You must be my friend Gaylord's housekeeper. Strange I never heard your name! Perhaps you have changed it?

Hester. No; 'twas a good name, given me by an honorable man. I have not soiled, so should not blush to bear it.

Thorpe. Indeed! Well, you know I could make this place too hot for you?

Hester. Could you? Try it.

Thorpe. A whisper to Gaylord, and the house-keeper's place would be vacant.

Hester. Do not leave your friend in the dark. Give him your confidence, your advice. Be an *honorable* counsellor — you are so fitted for it.

Thorpe. Hester Thorne, beware! Do not tempt me to crush you! On one condition I am silent. Let not that girl Grace know we have met before.

Hester. Condition? No; I will make no bargain with a villain. Do your worst. I have the courage — weak woman that you judge me — to fight you there — the power to win.

Thorpe. Enough. I know my duty to my friend; be assured I shall perform it.

(*Enter* AMOS L., *with a valise in hand.*)

Amos. Thorpe, I come to beg your pardon for a most inhospitable act. I am called away suddenly; have five minutes to catch the stage; may be gone two or three days. Make yourself at home here, and trust your comfort to Mrs. Thorne. Good-bye (*shakes hands with him*). Good-bye, Mrs. Thorne (*shakes hands with her, then goes up*).

Thorpe. But, Gaylord, one word.

Amos (*comes down*). Well, be quick; I've no time to lose.

Thorpe. Well — (*looks at* MRS. THORNE; *she smiles and goes up stage to table.*) Amos, you believe me to be your friend?

Amos. Certainly.

Thorpe. That woman there is dangerous.

Amos (whistles). You don't mean it? Well, Thorpe, do you know, I've just begun to think so?

Thorpe. I've met her before. She is not what she seems. She's a deserted wife.

Amos. Is she, poor thing?

Thorpe. Deserted by her husband, and not without cause. I could tell you a story.

Amos. But I haven't time. Goodness gracious! how my legs will have to fly now!

Thorpe. And you will trust that woman here after what I have told you?

Amos. Certainly. Why not, Thorpe? I'm surprised at you — a man of the world, you know. She's a good housekeeper, and — and — the rest is my secret (*with mock pomposity*). The mysteries of my "simple, honest country life"—ahem!—can scarcely interest you — the man of intrigue, you know. Don't be frightened, she won't hurt. Good-bye (*goes up*). Ah, Mrs. Thorne, I believe I forgot to shake hands with you (*gives hand*).

Hester. A pleasant journey, sir.

Amos. Thank you. Take good care of yourself (*with a look at* THORPE). I know you'll care for the comfort of my guest, for I have every confidence in you; nothing could shake that. Good-bye (*runs off c.*).

Thorpe. Curse that woman! she has bewitched him (*goes R.*).

Hester (coming down L.). Well, Mr. Thorpe, it seems your power to harm me here is weak.

[*Exit door* L.

Thorpe. Time will tell.

(*Enter* GRACE *and* LUCRETIA, *arm in arm,* R.)

Lucretia. Perfectly enchanting! I had no idea the country could be — so romantic! O, Mr. Thorpe, I have had such an Arcadian ramble in the farm-yard, seeing the little chickens running about with the *abandon* of children; the fatherly roosters with their clarion chorus; and the motherly biddies, with their careful affection for their young. Even the swine in their rustic abode, with the little pink-nosed pigs frolicking about them, was a delicious picture — so romantic! (*Goes to lounge.*)

Phil (*outside*). Not for me — not for me. There's freedom without. I'll be none of your hot-house flowers. Good-bye.

Grace. Ah! there's Crazy Phil. I've lured him in once; I'll try it again.

Thorpe. Shall I never get a word with her?

Grace (*at door; smiles off*). He sees me. Yes, I triumph. He's here. (PHIL *runs up to* C. *with gun.*)

Phil. Ah, those bright eyes again! There's magic in their glance. Wife — child — home — come back to this desolate heart!

Thorpe. Ah! (*Aside*) Brought to light at last. (*Aloud*) Crazy Phil indeed! Ha, ha, ha!

Phil (*starts*). Ah, that voice! 'Tis he — the destroyer! Years come and go, but fate holds the lines of life. We meet at last, — despoiler of my home! Wretch accursed! Death to thee! Death to thee! (*Raises gun.*)

Grace. No, no. (*Runs down to* THORPE *and throws*

arms about his neck.) He's mad! he's mad! (How-
ARD *enters door* C., *seizes* PHIL *around waist, and
snatches gun.*)

Howard. Madman, hold!

Phil (struggling to free himself). Away! He's
mine — he's mine! Foul bird of prey! you feasted at
my hearth-stone; you plucked from out my heart my
life! my love! Henceforth you are marked; my aim
is sure. Beware of Phil Thorne!

(*Enter* MRS. THORNE, L.)

Hester. Phil! — my husband! (*Falls with her arm
and head in arm-chair.*)

TABLEAU. PHIL *at door* C., *his clenched hand raised.*
HOWARD, *with arm about waist, holding him back.*
THORPE R. GRACE, *with arms about his neck, head
on his breast.* HESTER *lying with her head in arm-
chair.* LUCRETIA *on lounge, looking on.*

[*Slow Curtain.*]

ACT II.—SCENE: *Same as in* ACT I. *Easel removed from the stage. Foot of lounge turned toward window,* R. *Moonlight through window strong on* PHIL, *who lies upon lounge, boots changed for slippers.* HOWARD *standing at head of lounge, leaning against flat, his hand on* PHIL'S *head.* HESTER *standing behind window in flat, looking in at* PHIL. *Footlights down. Music soft and low at rising of curtain.*

Phil. How grandly the moonlight tips my old hut above the clouds! Dear old place; would I were there, where all is peace. Ah, Howard, when I descend that mountain, I leave behind my better self. The sight of the habitations of man awakes bitter memories of wrong and outrage, fill me with loathing of my race, and stir my baser nature with fierce desires for revenge. Why is it? Here I am always under the clouds; dark, dismal night forever here.

Howard. And yet the moonlight lingers as lovingly about you here as there. See how it floods the fields and shimmers on the stream. Ah, Phil, 'tis a beautiful world — this of ours; and, whether on the mountain-top or in the valley, robed in light or darkness at the desire of our own hearts.

Phil. That's queer philosophy!

Howard. 'Tis the truth, Phil. I am young and buoyant; life has gone smoothly for me, and all is

light.   You have suffered — still suffer; and the darkness of night has fallen upon your heart, blinding your
eyes to all the beauty about you.   Am I not right?

Phil.   Why am I lying here, Howard?

Howard.   I am glad to hear you ask that, Phil. 'Tis
three days since you were suddenly prostrated.   You
remember the day we went gunning — Monday?

Phil.   Yes.

Howard.   On our return you were suddenly taken
ill, and until this afternoon you were unconscious.

Phil.   Yes.   Well, I'm better now.   But why was
I taken ill?

Howard.   Well, you don't care to know that, Phil?

Phil.   You need not pause, Howard.   I know I
met here under your roof my wife and — and —

Howard.   Mr. Thorpe.

Phil.   Under the same roof, — he, the false, — and
she, the faithless!   O, Howard that man — that fiend!
Where is he?   Did I slay him?

Howard.   He is gone; where, I know not.

Phil (*starting to his feet*).   No matter; I'd reach
him, were he at the centre of the earth.   Curse him!
I thought long years had dulled my spirit; but the
sight of him has aroused the avenging demon in my
soul, nought but his life can satisfy.   (*Goes to* R.)

Howard (*comes down* L.).   No, no, Phil; forget your
wrongs; forgive your enemy.

Phil (R.).   Forgive him?   Howard, that man was
my dearest friend.   We both loved one woman.   She
chose me; and he, clasping my hand, wished me happiness, and fled abroad, to crush out his passion.   Well,

his wish was fulfilled. I was happy, supremely happy. Wife and child — two golden links in life's chain — were mine. Then he returned, still my friend. With full faith in his friendship, I received him a welcome guest in my home. Then, then, over the sunshine of my life rolled the dark clouds. He was one of your society-men — glib of tongue, ready to fetch and carry at the glance of a bright eye; all smiles and pretty ways — bah! a ladies' man — while I was brusque and sometimes rough, — though not to her — no, not to her. (*Crosses to* R.) I saw she was pleased at his attentions.

Howard. And you were jealous?

Phil. Not then. But one day I saw him slip a note into her hand; another; caught him at her feet; and then, filled with fury, I followed him from the house to his hotel, and there faced him and demanded an explanation. Then, Howard, that man, — my friend, trembling in every limb, with tears streaming down his cheeks, — confessed to me that he still loved my wife; and more, that she loved him; showed me letters signed with the name I gave her, confessing her mistake in making me her choice. In maddening rage I felled him to the floor and fled — fled to my now unhappy home (*comes to* L.).

Howard. And your wife?

Phil. Lay sleeping sweetly with a smile upon her lips, my child beside her. I raised my hand with passion, to dash out of that face the beauty that had so deceived me. But I could not do it. I snatched the child from its mother's side, and went out into the night — night to me for evermore.

Howard. Without a word from your wife, Phil? Condemned her you had sworn to love, cherish, and protect? Crazy Phil indeed! You were a madman then!

Phil. Had I not proofs? Her letters — the confession of my friend?

Howard. Friend? Base coward that he was! False to her; false to you! One word of denial from her lips — the wife of your bosom, the mother of your child — should have outweighed his guilty confession a thousand-fold. Tell me, Phil — you sought her afterwards?

Phil. No, never; since that night we have been strangers. Never met until I found them here together. You hear, Howard, — together here!

Howard. A mere accident. Mrs Thorne is our housekeeper. Thorpe, my father's friend and guest.

Phil. Ah, you know not that man — this woman!

Howard. I know no woman base enough to betray a loving husband's confidence. I will not believe this of her whom I respect and honor as I did my mother. Phil, you must meet her here, listen to the story from her lips.

Phil. No, I will not meet her. I will back to my hut above the clouds.

Howard. And leave her still under the cloud that has saddened her life. O, Phil! Phil! I thought you true and noble.

Phil. Think what you will. Wronged by my friend, betrayed by my wife, I have lost all worth living for.

(*Fiercely.*) I hate the world ; I hate myself! Let me go! — there — there — (*totters*).

Howard (*supporting him*). Not to-night, Phil. You are weak, ill. Forgive me; it was cruel in me to probe those angry wounds. Come back to your room. We are friends still, Phil.

Phil (*taking his hand*). Heaven bless you, Howard! I've none but you now. Don't speak ; something in your words has stirred me strangely. Be silent ; let me think ; let me rest. (*Music soft ;* PHIL *leads him off door* L. HESTER *comes down slowly,* C., *watching the door.*)

Hester. I have heard his voice ; unobserved listened to his story. How he has misconceived my actions, Heaven, myself, and he the wily plotter alone know. He confessed with tears in his eyes, 'base hypocrite! O, Phil, my husband — lost to me! He shall confess once more ; confess the truth — the honest truth, to do me justice. Fool that I have been! I have allowed suspicion to crush me to the earth, without one effort to clear my name. Now my woman's nature is in arms against this base injustice (*comes to* R.). I am not friendless ; those true-hearted sons of the soil — Heaven bless them! — believe me, trust me. They have given me courage to seek the weakness in this villain's armor. Hester, be brave, be resolute, and victory may yet be yours. [*Exit* R. 1 E.

(*Enter* GRACE, C.)

Grace. O dear! for the first time I feel really homesick! There's no pleasure in roaming in the

moonlight alone; it requires two to take in the full
beauty of a night like this! Heigho! I miss my usual
escort. (*Takes book from table, and goes to lounge;
sits.*) Whittier. (*Opens book.*) "Howard Gaylord."
So, so — my farmer friend is an admirer of our New
England poet. It's been well thumbed, too, especially
"Among the Hills." (*Reads.*)

> "From school, and ball, and rout, she came,
>   The city's fair, pale daughter,
> To drink the wine of mountain air,
>   Beside the Bearcamp Water."

That's splendid! my own favorite, — and it seems to
be his too. The leaves are dog-eared, and the page
muddy with finger marks. O,

> "The city's fair, pale daughter,"

must be very dear to him. I wonder if in his heart-
picture she bears any resemblance to me? O, here he
is! (*Reads.*)

(*Enter* HOWARD, *door* L.)

Howard (*aside*). Reading in the moonlight. What
a pretty picture she makes! Alone — there's a temp-
tation. If I only had the gift of tongue that graces her
city admirers, I might — well — say that which would
make us strangers. I could not bear her scorn.
(*Aloud*) Reading by moonlight? Take care, Miss
Grace; even the brightness of *your* eyes may be
dimmed.

Grace (*looking up*). Ah, Mr. Gaylord, there's no
danger: 'tis as light as noonday.

Howard. The book must be very interesting that can so attract you.

Grace. It is. I am "Among the Hills," and you step in very *apropos.*

Howard. "Among the Hills?" Then you are in that region of the unequalled poet's fancy, where I most delight to wander.

Grace. I should think so by the appearance of your book. Were you a boy at school, you would get many bad marks for the very bad marks you have placed upon it.

Howard. I am a boy at school, Miss Grace — the school of the painter. Will you teach me?

Grace. I? I am but a scholar. You know the poem?

Howard. By heart. I could repeat it word for word.

Grace. 'Tis very odd you should have dropped in just at this time, for I was reading. (*Reads.*)

> " She sat beneath the broad-armed elms
> That skirt the mowing-meadow,
> And watched the gentle west-wind weave
> The grass with shine and shadow."

Now here 's where you came in :

> " Beside her, from the summer heat
> To share her grateful screening,
> With forehead bared, the farmer stood,
> Upon his pitchfork leaning."

Only you haven't the pitchfork.

Howard. Go on. I could listen to you all night ; you throw so much heart into it.

Grace. Do I? (*Reads.*)

> " Framed in its damp, dark locks, his face
> ·Had nothing mean or common, —
> Strong, manly, true, the tenderness
> And pride beloved of woman.

> " She looked up, glowing with the health
> The country air had brought her,
> And, laughing, said, ' You lack a wife,
> Your mother lacks a daughter.

> " ' To mend your frock and bake your bread
> You do not need a lady;
> Be sure among these brown old homes
> Is some one waiting ready.' "

Grace. O, I forgot you have no mother! But the rest
is true.   There is "some one waiting ready."

Howard.   In "these brown old homes"? No, I am
free to take up the burden of the lay. (*Recites with
spirit.*)

> " He bent his black brows to a frown,
> He set his white teeth tightly.
> ' 'Tis well,' he said, ' for one like you
> To choose for me so lightly.

> " ' You think me deaf and blind; you bring
> Your winning graces hither
> As free as if from cradle-time
> We two had played together.

> " ' You tempt me with your laughing eyes,
> Your cheeks of sundown's blushes,
> A motion as of waving grain,
> A music as of thrushes.

> " ' No mood is mine to seek a wife,
>   Or daughter for my mother;
> Who loves you loses in that love
>   All power to love another!

> " ' I dare your pity or your scorn,
>   With pride your own exceeding;
> ·I fling my heart into your lap

(*Kneels at her feet.*)

> Without a word of pleading.' "

O, Grace, Grace, it is the truth. I love you, and you alone. (*Takes her hand.*)

Grace. Why, that's not in the poem.

Howard. No; it is in my heart.

Grace. (*Looks at him archly; places her hand in his.*) It's a pity to spoil the poem. (*Recites.*)

> ." She looked up in his face of pain
>   So archly, yet so tender:
> ' And if I lend you mine,' she said,
>   ' Will you forgive the lender ?

> " ' Nor frock nor tan can hide the man;
>   And see you not, my farmer,
> How weak and fond a woman waits
>   Behind this silken armor?

(*Puts her hand on his shoulder, and looks down into his eyes.*)

> " ' I love you; on that love alone,
>   And not my worth, presuming,
> Will you not trust for summer fruit
>   The tree in May-day blooming? ' "

Howard, as frankly as you offered, as freely will I re-

10

ceive, yours — yours alone. (*Kisses his brow.* **Both rise.**)

Howard. Ah, Grace, Grace ; you have made me very happy. (*Puts his arm about her waist.*) Come, let's go into the garden.

Grace.
 " And so the farmer found a wife,
 His mother found a daughter ;
 There looks no happier home than **hers**
 On pleasant Bearcamp Water."

Howard. Ah, Grace, Heaven bless the dear poet.

Grace. It does, " for all his works do praise him." (*They pass off through the window* R., *his arm about her waist.*)

(*Enter* NAT, C., *with* SUSY *leaning on his arm.*)

Susy. Why, Mr. Naylor, what's the matter with you? You have not made a rhyme for the last hour.

Nat. The minstrel's strings are mute ; the fire upon the altar of poesy smoulders ; the theme which agitates my brain respectfully declines to shape itself for utterance — because why ?

Susy. Well, perhaps the strings are rotten, the wood green, and the theme too weighty ?

Nat. O, for seraphic light to break the gloom.

Susy. Wouldn't moonlight do as well ? There's plenty of it here (*sits on lounge*).

Nat (*standing* C.)

 Cold Luna floods thee with her silvery light,
 O, beauteous maid, ne'er saw I fairer sight.

Susy (*aside*). The wood is sizzling on the altar ;

we'll soon have another blaze. (*Aloud*) Don't be so distant. Come, sit down. (NAT *sits.*) Now what is this mighty theme?

Nat. 'Tis Love — ecstatic Love.

Susy. O!

Nat. I wander up and down in strange unrest,
For love is struggling — is struggling —

Susy. Underneath my vest. That's good.

Nat. O, no, no.

Susy. Ha, ha, ha! That's what I call clothing a sentiment in warm language. Well, what next?

Nat. Nothing. There it struggles, there it sticks. O, Susy, Susy, I'm getting —

Susy. Boozy. That's a capital rhyme.

Nat. Miss Susy Gaylord, you shock me!

Susy. Do I? That's a shocking confession when I'm doing my best to help you. I told you I would. Now, isn't that moon splendid? See the trees yonder, with leaves of silver (*both look off* R.).

(*Enter* CHIPS, C.)

Chips (*at door*). I was just going by. Ah, there they are billing and cooing like a couple of lunatics. (*Creeps down stage to arm-chair, turns it round so that back is towards* NAT; *gets on his knees in it, and watches them over the top while speaking.*) I'm blowed if I don't hear what's going on. I ain't going to be cut out with Susy without a wrestle.

Nat. A fairy scene. It moves me, thrills me; my heart heaves with bliss.

Chips (*aside*). Well, clap on a little mustard, and make it blister.

Nat. And see those fairy forms moving among the trees.

Chips (aside). Fairy forms? I'm darned if Gaylord's pigs ain't got loose again.

Nat. Ah, for a poet's home in that delightful grove, with an angel ever at my side — that angel you.

Susy. Law, Mr. Naylor, how you do go on; first Chips calls me an angel, and now you.

Nat. Chips? Mention not that rustic booby.

Chips. Booby! (*Gets out of chair; starts towards* NAT, *then runs back.*)

Susy (rises indignantly). Booby! How dare you call my friend such a name!

Nat. It is the truth : he is a rough, uncouth booby. I know he seeks to gain your love. But when I, with my pure, poetic nature, tell you — sweet and beautiful damsel — that your charms have kindled a flame in this before obdurate heart; that I love you —

Susy. No more, sir. Booby indeed! Curtis Chipman is far above you in manhood, nobility, and goodness. He is rough and uncouth as the rocky soil he with his strong hands has made to bring forth abundant fruits. A man, sir, and not a maudlin idiot filled with gush and moonshine. (*Comes down* R.)

Nat (goes to c.). And have I been deceived in you? you, whose poetic nature, blending with mine —

Susy. Has sported with you. Yes. O, Mr. Naylor, go back to your attic. Live in the clouds; feed on Poesy's hills — you'll find no mate in me.

Nat. Alas! I am deceived! My heart is crushed — My spirit broken —

Susy. And your verses mushed!
Ha, ha, ha! Good-bye, my poet. We might have been
good friends; but when you attack Chips — my Chips —

The rustic booby, really I must laugh,
For I propose to be his better half.

Impromptu. Ahem!

Nat. Farewell, cold Susy, I have wooed in vain!

Susy. You have; your wood is green and crossed in
grain.

Impromptu. Ahem!

Nat (at door, c.). Farewell. I'm blasted — blasted.
[*Exit* c.

Chips (aside). I'm a blasted liar if I don't wal-
lop him! (*Runs up and catches* Susy *in his arms;
swings her round.*) O, Susy, Susy — you *are* an angel!
(Susy *screams;* Chips *runs off* c.)

Susy. Well, I never! Chips has heard all. There's
no more fun for me. Dear me, I've forgotten Mr. Turtle's hourly lunch! He'll be raving and starving too.
[*Exit door* L.

(*Enter,* c., Turtle *with* Miss Lucretia *on his arm.*)

Lucretia. So kind of you, Mr. Turtle, to wander
with me in the beautiful night; it quite fills an aching
void — so romantic.

Turtle (aside). It gives me an aching void — so
hungry.

Lucretia (going towards window). Is this the
'witching hour of night,' which the poet so beautifully
speaks of?

Turtle. Can't say (*looking at his watch*). It's my
hour for lunch.

Lucretia (sits on lounge). What a delightful situation; moonbeams shrouding me as in a silver veil! Ah, I've often dreamed of such an hour as this — a scene like this — when the future partner of my joys and sorrows should claim me for his own — so romantic.

Turtle (aside). Well, she lives on dreams. I'm glad I don't.

Lucretia. He must be one who would love me for myself alone, and not for my money.

Turtle (aside.) Has the old girl got money? (*Aloud.*) O Miss Lucretia, could there live a wretch who, looking upon your charms, would dare to woo you for your fortune? (*Aside.*) That's neat and non-committal. (*Aloud.*) And yet, your fortune renders you independent of all suitors. A few thousands —

Lucretia. A few? I can count by tens of thousands!

Turtle (aside). Tens? She's a rich old girl. What dinners! — what suppers! (*Approaching her tenderly.*) My dear Miss Lucretia, what would be hundreds of thousands to the man who, knowing your virtues, basking in your smiles, should be so fortunate as to win you?

Lucretia. Then you believe in love, Mr. Turtle; pure, genuine love, that scorns wealth and station?

Turtle. Unbounded love! Yes, Lucretia (*sits beside her*).

Lucretia. Love and a cottage — so romantic.

Turtle. Yes, Lucretia. (*Aside.*) Love-cake and cottage-pudding.

Lucretia. With innocent lambs sporting about the door.

Turtle. Yes, Lucretia. (*Aside*) Or smoking on the table.

Lucretia. And the birds — What is your favorite bird?

Turtle. My favorite bird? (*Aside*) Quail on toast. (*Aloud*) The cook — O, dear Miss Lucretia.

Lucretia. And your favorite flower?

Turtle (*aside*). Best Family. (*Aloud*) The *Marry* gold, Miss Lucretia.

Lucretia. And your favorite seat?

Turtle (*aside*). At the dinner-table. (*Aloud*) Under the oak, Lucretia.

Lucretia. And your favorite vegetable?

Turtle (*aside*). Rare dishes. (*Aloud*) I could not turn up my nose at any of them, Miss Lucretia.

Lucretia. Ah, what taste you have — so romantic. This is my dream of bliss — a cottage and a companion — bonds of affection and notes of gladness.

. *Turtle.* My heart echoes the glad refrain. (*Aside*) Government bonds and bank notes.

Lucretia. What a delightful picture — so romantic.

Turtle (*aside*). Such a picture should have a gold frame. (*Aloud*) Dear Miss Lucretia, could you look with favor on me — share your tens of thousands —

Lucretia. Romantic visions, castles in the sky; so ethereal; so much more to be enjoyed than palaces of earth — my wealth, my all. What care I for the well-filled purse which another squanders? I am poor in lucre, but a millionnaire in love. O, Titus, spare my blushes! Yes — (*Leans upon his shoulder.*)

Turtle (aside). She's poor as porridge. Here's a scrape.

Lucretia. O, Titus, " Whisper what thou feelest." So romantic in the moonshine.

Turtle (aside). Hang it, it's all moonshine. (*Aloud*) Lucretia, I feel — I feel — (*aside*) hungry

Lucretia. I have so longed for this delicious moment.

Turtle (aside). No doubt of it. (*Aloud*) Miss Lucretia, when I asked you to look with favor upon me, I felt how unworthy I was of your affection ; how badly fitted I am to become your protector. This slender frame —

Lucretia. What care I for the frame; it's the treasure within I covet — the heart, Titus — the heart. Nothing shall tear me from you !

(*Enter* SUSY, L., *with candles, which she places on table.*)

Turtle (aside). O, here's a situation.

Susy (aside). I declare! Making love! I'll spoil that. (*Aloud*) Your lunch is ready — cold shoulder of mutton.

Turtle (jumps up). O glorious signal of relief!

Lucretia. O, Titus, you will not leave me in this delicious moment ?

Turtle. For that delicious shoulder I must, Lucretia. My heart says stay ; my stomach says go. The mighty always conquer the weak. I'd offer thee this hand of mine, if I could — could — banish the cold shoulder, — if I could inhabit your airy castles. But look at my size ; look at my waist! I cannot feed on love. Farewell ; be happy with another ; I've not the least objection. I'll do the same; I'll be happy with another. (*Aside*) The cold shoulder.   [*Exit* L.

Lucretia. The wretch! — the gourmand! the — O! desert me for a cold shoulder! — me, who has reposed upon his warm shoulder! O, I could cry — but I won't. I'll wander like a spectre amid the trees, broken-hearted. So romantic.   [*Exit through window.*

Susy. Now, I wonder where she's going at this time of night? (*Goes to window.*) O my goodness! There's Chips and that Naylor chap stripping off their coats out there in the pasture! I do believe they're going to fight! Chips! Chips!

[*Exit through window.*

(*Enter* PHIL, *door* L.)

Phil. I cannot rest. When I close my eyes, the sleeping face of my wife comes before me as I saw it that night, as innocent in its expression as the child's that slept beside her. Have I been mistaken? Have I all these years been fighting a demon of my own conjuring? — all these years, with no confidant, blindly treading the path of error? This boy — with his chivalrous honor, makes me blush with shame. He loves her, esteems her, — she who was to him a stranger but a few short months ago ; — while I, with her life knit to mine by the tenderest tie, have blasted her name, made her a creature to be shunned, by my base desertion of her, — perhaps without cause. I'll not be hasty, but I will hear the story from her lips.

Perhaps — perhaps — O, Heavens! if she is innocent — what am I? A wretch too base to live. Let me not think of that. If she be innocent, how gladly would I die to clear her name (*slowly crosses stage and exits through window, R.*).

Amos (outside). Hallo! Susy! Howard! Mrs. Thorne! (*Enters c.*) Well, well, well! The house deserted; nobody to welcome me, its master, when he brings such glorious tidings. Ah, here's some one at last.

(*Enter from window,* GRACE *and* HOWARD ; *from* R. 1 E. HESTER.)

Howard. Ah, father, welcome home (*shakes hands*).

Amos. Well, how are you? And my little painter friend? (*Shakes hands with* GRACE.) Mrs. Thorne, I'm glad to meet you again. (*Shakes hands with her.*)

Hester. You must be tired and hungry.

Amos. Hungry? Why, I'm famishing; and so is my horse. Howard, take care of him.

Howard. At once, sir. (*Exit c.* GRACE *sits on lounge.*)

Hester (going to door L.). I will see that your supper is prepared.

Amos. Not just yet. Mrs. Thorne, I have been absent in your interests. Are you not anxious to know the result?

Hester. I am more anxious for your comfort, sir. I told you it were better to let the past rest.

Amos. Yes; three days ago you surprised me with the story of that past. I told you I would be your friend. I come to-night to surprise you.

Hester. · Surprise me?

Amos. Yes. Your daughter lives !

Hester. No, no, it is impossible; she died years ago. I learned it —

Amos. From a newspaper report. It was a lie; a forgery; wrought by a cunning hand to keep you from your child.

Hester. O, Mr. Gaylord, can it be? Shall I see her again? O, dear, dear friend, tell me all.

Grace (rising). Your pardon; you do not desire company, and I will —

Amos. Stay where you are, Grace. This story may interest you, as showing to what extent villany may be carried by so unscrupulous a man as Alfred Thorpe.

Hester. Alfred Thorpe!

Grace. My guardian!

Amos. Mrs. Thorne, the story of your wrongs made a deep impression upon me. I was quick to catch any suspicious circumstance, and from his own lips I gained the information that led me to believe he was the traitorous friend.

Hester. He was; he was.

Amo·. Then his fat friend, Turtle, in an angry moment gave me another hint, which I was not slow to take advantage of. I took the stage, and yesterday alighted at a pleasant little place forty miles from here, called Greenland. There I hunted up an old friend of your husband. From him I learned that your husband had left a child with him years ago; gave it to him to be taken care of; to be given up if called for, — otherwise, to live and die as his child. From that day to this he has never seen the father; but three years after, a man bearing an order came for the child and took it away.

Hester. And that is all?

Amos. No ; that is but the beginning. I traced the child to its new home ; traced the report of its death ; picked up straggling threads in the child's life; the name of its father; the name of the bearer of the order; until I proved conclusively that your child is alive and well.

Hester. O, Mr. Gaylord, can I find her? can I clasp her in my arms?

Amos. Hester (*taking her hand*), as I believe in truth and justice, believe me, the words I am about to speak are the truth, truth beyond a doubt. The child that bore the name of Grace Thorne now bears the name of Grace Ingalls (*goes down* R.).

Grace. O, mother, mother! (*Runs into* HESTER's *arms.*)

Hester (*clasping her in her arms*). My child! My dear, dear child!

Amos. Well, it strikes me that "rough country life " is looking up.

Grace. O, I am so happy! No earthly name is so dear as that of " mother! "

Hester. Save that of " child." Grace, my darling, I feel this must be a reality, — so much in your face that has attracted me grows into the likeness of the babe torn from me, that I cannot doubt.

Grace. And I catch the same tenderness in your loving eyes that has been to me a blessed memory for years! O, mother, mother! there is so much love springing to new life in my heart, there is no room for doubt.

Amos (*crossing to door* L., *behind*). Now, having satisfactorily reported the results of my journey, with your leave, ladies, I will now satisfy the cravings of my appetite.

Hester. I will attend you, sir.

Amos. No, no; I will not interrupt you.

Hester. Nay, I insist. You have been so kind to me, Mr. Gaylord — such a dear friend — (*gives her hand*) I know not how to recompense you.

Amos. Well, suppose you give me a cup of tea. After you, madam. (*Opens door, steps back and bows.* HESTER *goes to door, then turns, stops a minute, runs* C. *and embraces* GRACE, *then runs off door* L. AMOS, *about to go, turns and looks at* GRACE.)

Grace (*runs and throws her arms about his neck*). Heaven bless you, dear Mr. Gaylord; you have made me very, very happy.

Amos (*kissing her forehead*). Serves you right. (*Aside*) I'd like to be a second father to that girl. Ah, well, if I've made them happy, I must be content.

[*Exit door* L.

Grace. Dear old man, how I love him! That's a very proper sentiment too, for he's Howard's father; and if —

(*Enter* THORPE, C.)

Thorpe. Grace, — Grace, my darling (*comes down* R. *with outstretched hands ; she starts back to* L.).

Grace. Mr. Thorpe!

Thorpe. Why this coldness? Have they turned you against me? Has my enforced absence shocked you? I could not help it; the sight of that man who has basely wronged me —

Grace. Spare your apologies, I beg, Mr. Thorpe. You are master of your own actions. No one has been surprised at your absence. Why should I be?

Thorpe. Grace, you know how dear you are to me. No, I am wrong; you cannot. I have watched you from childhood with all a father's care. You have grown into beautiful womanhood; and with no paternal blood to check the feeling, a strong and tender love has taken the place of fatherly interest. Grace Ingalls, I love you with the one mighty passion of my life. Will you become my wife?

Grace. No, no; do not press me. I owe you much; my heart is filled with gratitude for your tender care.

Thorpe. You have much cause to be grateful. I have freely lavished upon you wealth, and made you renowned. These should make you ponder well ere you refuse the boon I ask.

Grace. Mr. Thorpe, when three days ago you broached this subject to my great surprise, I weighed well my duty and my inclination. I appreciate all your goodness; thank you a thousand times for all your care; and could I repay you —

Thorpe. You can; you must; — with your love.

Grace. Impossible. Within an hour my life has wondrously changed. Mr. Thorpe, I have often asked you to tell me of my parents — of my father.

Thorpe. I have told you — he is dead.

Grace. And my mother?

Thorpe. She, too, is dead (*aside*) to you.

Grace. And this, you tell me, is the truth; on your honor?

Thorpe. On my honor.

Grace. And you ask me to marry you? Mr. Thorpe, with your words still ringing in my ears, I refer you to one who alone has the right to dispose of my hand. (*Points to* HESTER, *who enters door* L.) My mother. (HOWARD *appears* C.)

Thorpe (*starts and goes* R.). Her mother! (*Aside*) Whose fiendish work is this?

(HOWARD *comes down;* GRACE *takes his arm, and they pass off through window,* R.)

Hester. You hear, Alfred Thorpe: that girl, pure and innocent, calls me mother.

Thorpe. She has no right.

Hester. 'Tis useless to deny what can be fully proved. Every link in the chain of evidence, from the time you kidnapped my child, has been fully tested by Amos Gaylord.

Thorpe. Amos Gaylord?

Hester. Yes; the man whom you sought to turn against me has outwitted you. With all your cunning, the honest, simple-hearted farmer has wrought the good work which gives the mother to her child again.

Thorpe. And you triumph! How? You have snatched the girl from her home — a life of ease and luxury — for what? To share the hard fate of a suspected and despised woman.

Hester. Suspected? Yes. Despised? No. True, warm friends have gathered about me in my darkest hour. I am strong in my own innocence, and shall live down the distrust which you alone have created. Ay, more, I stand between you and the woman you love. We have changed places, Alfred Thorpe, for I now have the power to make your life as miserable as you have made mine.

Thorpe. But you will not. Hester, I love that girl; dearly, madly love her. Give her to me. Let all that has passed be forgotten. I will make any reparation you may ask; only give her to me. See (*kneels*), on my knees I ask this precious boon.

Hester. On your knees — Ah! (Phil, *with his arms folded, his eyes on the ground as if in deep thought, enters from window* R., *and passes out through door* C., Hester *looking at him.* Thorpe *has his head bowed, and does not see him. Aside*) Let me be firm. (*Aloud*) Alfred Thorpe — (Phil *is just passing the window* L. C. ; *he starts, stops, and watches through window*) — once, trembling in every limb, and with tears streaming down your cheeks, you made a confession to my husband. Are you now prepared to confess to me?

Thorpe (*rising*). What shall I confess?

Hester. The truth. If you hope for my consent — if you hope for mercy hereafter — tell me, why have you so bitterly pursued me?

Thorpe. Because I loved you, Hester. I could not bear to see you the wife of that man, Philip Thorne. You chose him. From that moment I determined you should be mine. I would break the chain that bound you to him. 'Twas easily done : a few forged letters, a few startling situations, and the fool believed you guilty, and deserted you.

Hester. Did I not spurn you from me, and treat with contempt your base proposals ?

Thorpe. You did; and when I had succeeded in separating you from your husband, when I believed that you could be made to love me, having no protector, I found I had deceived myself, and you were a pure and noble woman. O, Hester, I am a fool to let my tongue betray me now ; but on your words hangs my fate. I thought I loved you as I could never love another; but she who is now the image of what you once was has aroused a mightier passion in my breast, and the love which was once yours, a thousand-fold deepened, goes out to her, your daughter.

Hester. And what reparation do you propose for me, the woman you have robbed of her husband, branded with suspicion, and degraded in the eyes of the world ?

Thorpe. Ample, Hester. Grace my wife, our house is yours. Beneath my roof an honored guest, the past will be forgotten as an idle tale, and all the future filled with peace and happiness.

Hester. And my husband ?

Thorpe. Poor fool ! let him be forgotten. He never loved you. Think you that, had I been lifted to your love, I should have allowed suspicion to break my trust in you ? No, no ; he was no true man. Let him rest here among the hills. Weak in intellect, enfeebled

11

in body, he will soon pass away, and, like your wrongs, be as soon forgotten.

Hester. And you ask me to give you my daughter? Alfred Thorpe, you are a villain! The murderer who lifts his hand against his brother man is a hero, yea, a saint, compared with a coward who, like you, lifts his voice to sully a woman's reputation! I'd rather see my child again lost to me — lost forever! — than have her become the mate of such as you! (*Crosses to* R.)

Thorpe. Yet I will have her! Mark me, Hester, she shall be mine! I have stooped to you; I will again, — but it shall be as the eagle stoops to seize its prey! Remember, you are an outcast. The breath of suspicion, like the foul miasma, once it blasts the atmosphere about a woman, cannot easily be shaken off. You are weak and friendless; I, strong and powerful. Once I set my schemes afoot, I pause not till I conquer. I will not now. I'll have your daughter. You may struggle and writhe, — proclaim your innocence, but who — who will believe you?

Phil (*rushing on,* C.). I will — I, Philip Thorne. (*Stands* C., *with right hand raised.* THORPE L. *of* C.) Right, Alfred Thorpe, he was no true man; he was a fool. But now the light is breaking in on his weak intellect; the clouds are lifting. Enfeebled in body? Ha! (*Seizes* THORPE *by throat with left hand.*) Liar! But a few days ago, on a precipitous spur in yonder mountain, where but one could pass, I met a fierce and hungry bear, who clasped me in his arms. On the brink we struggled — he and I — in close embrace of life and death, my hand upon his throat, as now on

yours, I drove my knife into his heart, and flung him
to the abyss below. (*Lifts* THORPE, *and throws him
with right hand, on stage.*) Enfeebled — I? Ha, ha,
ha! (*Lifts his foot to trample on him.*)

(*Enter from window* R., GRACE *and* HOWARD; *by door
L.,* AMOS. HESTER *runs up and places her hand on*
PHIL'S *right shoulder.*)

Hester. Philip! (*Music, piano.* THORPE *rises and
goes to table.*)

Phil (*looking at her steadily*). Hester, innocent and
wronged one, dare I look thee in the face again? No,
no; on my knees, at your feet — (*about to kneel*).

Hester (*raising him quickly*) No, no, my husband;
all is forgotten, all forgiven. Take me to your arms;
tell me you believe me —

Phil (*clasping her in his arms*). Innocent! innocent! My own dear wife! (*Music stops.* THORPE
goes to door. C.)

Thorpe (*looking in*). They've won the game and
ruined me. But I held the reins for twelve long years!
Let them remember that. (*Goes off* L.; *stops at window and shakes fist.*) Remember that. [*Exit* L.

Hester. Dear Philip, that our union may be com-
plete, look upon our daughter. Grace, my child, your
father (*steps to* R.).

Grace (*running into* PHILIP'S *arms*). Father!

Phil. My child! The face did not deceive me; it
was Hester's — Hester's, as I knew it ere —

Hester (*goes to him on* R.). Ere the clouds obscured
it, Philip; but they've rolled away, and all is bright
again.

Phil. Wondrous bright. (*Left arm about* GRACE, *right arm about* HESTER; *looks first at one, then at the other.*) The skies are clear, and the stars of love are shining on my path.

Amos (R.). Mrs. Thorne, we have beaten the enemy at last.

Hester (*gives hand*). Thanks to you, dear, dear friend.

Amos (*crosses to* PHIL). Old boy, you're in luck (*gives his hand*). Your wife is a treasure; and your daughter —

Howard (*gives* PHIL *his hand*). An angel! Ah, Phil, you've truly found out the world is what we make it. I wish you joy.

Amos. I almost envy you. I wish that daughter was mine.

Howard. It will not be my fault if she is not, father.

Amos. Hallo! Hallo! What do you mean, sir? (GRACE *gives her hand to* HOWARD.) Ho, ho! I understand. Town and country have found out the truth that they cannot live without each other. (*All stand a little R. of C., near window, in a group talking.*)

Susy (*outside* C.). O dear! boo-hoo! — (*Crying.*) It's a shame!

(*Enter* SUSY, C., *with her apron to her eyes.*)

Amos. Hallo, Susy! What's the matter?

Susy. O dear! I — I — I — boo-hoo — think it's a shame — so it is.

Amos. So do I, Susy, whatever it is. Who's been plaguing you?

Susy. Chips — and — and — boo-hoo, Mr. Nay — Nay — Naylor — been — been fighting just awful.

Amos. Fighting? What about?

Susy. Me, sir! I — I — I tried to stop 'em, but — but — they wo — wo — wouldn't, and they're all bru — bruised.

(*Enter* NAT, c. ; *his clothes are torn ; his necktie hanging ; one eye blacked; one cheek puffed out ; face scratched, and hair ruffled. Comes down* R.)

Nat. Upon the moonlit plain we met as foes :
He blacked my eye — I flattened out his nose.

Impromptu. Ahem!

(*Enter* CHIPS, c., *in an equally forlorn condition, his nose bleeding, face scratched, &c. Both characters should present signs of having fought long and well.*)

Chips (*coming down* L.). Yes, darn you, you're a spunky chap, for all your loose rhymes.

Amos. What does this mean? Explain yourselves.

Chips. I ain't got nothin' to say. I was jest goin' by —

Susy. Now stop. Ain't you ashamed of yourself, Chips? (AMOS *goes back to group,* R.)

Chips. Don't care : he called me a booby.

Nat. I withdraw the appellation, Chips.

Susy. There! Now shake hands and be friends.

Chips. I don't want to.

Susy. You must. Come here, Mr. Naylor. (*Takes his hand and leads him over to* Chips, L.) Now shake hands. Confess you have made fools of yourselves, and become friends.

Nat (*holds out his hand*). I'm willing.

   Chip of a stubborn block, my dexter take —
   We will be friends —we will —

Chips. O, 'nuff said, — shake. (*They shake hands.*)

    (*Enter* Lucretia, R.)

Lucretia. Has anybody seen my Titus ?

(*Enter* Turtle *from door* L.., *a napkin about his neck, a huge slice of pie in one hand, and a piece of cheese in the other, eating.* Turtle *crosses stage; at the same time* Grace *goes to table* C., *and sits.* Susy *sits in arm-chair* L., *keeping up a dumb show of conversation with* Chips *on her right and* Nat *on her left.* Howard *goes up to vase of flowers in the passage.*)

Turtle. Were you looking for me, Miss Lucretia ?

Lucretia. Yes, Titus ; I was hungering for your society, thirsting for the music of your voice.

Turtle. Hungering and thirsting. Now, that's true poetry — the language of the appetite. So was I. Ah, Lucretia, the cold shoulder has done its work. While it assuaged my appetite, it filled my soul with remorse (*bites pie*). Forgive me, Lucretia, I have awakened to a realizing sense of your virtues (*bites cheese*). It brought to my mind the time when I sat at your table and partook of a hot shoulder cooked by your own fair hands. It was luscious! May I not hope that your fair hands may feed me — no, lead me — to many such feasts?

Lucretia.   O Titus, we may be happy yet. So romantic.

(PHIL *stands* R. C., *with his arm about* HESTER'S *waist, looking off* R. *Moonlight on them.* AMOS *comes down* C. HOWARD *comes down to table, with flowers in his hand.*)

Amos.   Well, Susy, are all your troubles over?

Susy.   Yes, father. Chips and I have made up our minds to — to —   You tell him, Chips.

Chips.   O, certainly. Mr. Gaylord, I was telling Susy — no, Susy was telling me. Well, I'll come in and tell you to-morrow, — when I'm going by.

Nat.   When going by, he'll lift the latch,
        To let you know they've made a match.

Impromptu. Ahem!

Amos.   Ha, ha! I see. Well, I shall be at home. (*Goes up* C.)   Phil, old fellow, why so silent?

Phil.   For wonder. Amos, an hour ago, life was a dreary waste to me. How quick the change. There a daughter, and here a wife — the golden links of long ago put on again to bind me willing captive!

Hester.   We are both to blame. Had we trusted in each other, all that has marred our lives we should have escaped. We have been taught the lesson of faith through trial and tribulation in the lost years. Reunited, we will take it to our hearts. Now all is bright again.

Phil. Bright as yonder peak, my home no longer. Hester, here in this bustling world below I'll rear again our happy home; and though the tempest has beaten about us, and darkness obscured our path, — with confidence and trust to lead and guide, with strength and courage to subdue, we will journey on. The gloom dispersed, the shadows rolled away, the light of love upon our pathway, with Heaven's help we will triumphantly lift ourselves — Above the Clouds.

TABLEAU. — PHIL R. C., *arm about* HESTER's *waist, right hand pointing off through window; moonlight on them.* AMOS *near door* C., *watching them.* GRACE *seated at table, looking up at* HOWARD, *who stands back of table and places flowers in her hair.* SUSY *in armchair* L., *with* CHIPS *leaning over it.* NAT *extreme* L., *with a pencil and note-book, scratching his head with pencil, as though trying to make a verse.* TURTLE *and* LUCRETIA *extreme* R., *arm in arm, looking at* PHIL.

[*Music, and Slow Curtain.*] .

www.ingramcontent.com/pod-product-compliance
Lightning Source LLC
Chambersburg PA
CBHW030009030726
47499CB00008B/2969